Good Witch, Bad Witch

RT Woods

Illustrated by
Bekah Crowmer

AuthorHouse™ UK Ltd.
1663 Liberty Drive
Bloomington, IN 47403 USA
www.authorhouse.co.uk
Phone: 0800.197.4150

Published by AuthorHouse

ISBN: 978-1-4969-8492-0 (sc)
ISBN: 978-1-4969-8493-7 (e)

Any people depicted in stock imagery provided by Thinkstock are models, and such images are being used for illustrative purposes only.
Certain stock imagery © Thinkstock.

This book is printed on acid-free paper.

Because of the dynamic nature of the Internet, any web addresses or links contained in this book may have changed since publication and may no longer be valid. The views expressed in this work are solely those of the author and do not necessarily reflect the views of the publisher, and the publisher hereby disclaims any responsibility for them.

author HOUSE

The Witches

Oh! The Witches

The beautiful Witches

Which spell shall you cast today?

What magic will you make tomorrow?

Good or Bad

Black or White,

May you live forever and a day

Never to be forgotten

In the shadows of the past

R.T. Woods

There once lived two witches

One good, one bad

Alone in their houses.

The Bad Witch had twenty rooms

Big and closed, full of dust and pungent air.

Spider webs spun from chair to chair.

For a friend she had a rat,

Black as night, with a long thin tail,

No name at all. She just called it Rat.

The Good Witch lived alone as well

In a very small house –

Two rooms with a study

For mixing potions and practicing spells.

The other room – kept well and clean,

For people to stay if the case did incline.

For a friend she had a dog

White and fluffy

With wagging tail – a smiling face.

Honey Dew was

This little dog called.

One day the Bad Witch woke up

Feeling sick, very ill.

Her teeth were loose,

One by one they began to fall.

She looked into her cracked mirror –

The wart on her nose

Seemed bigger with the gapping spaces

Where her teeth had fallen out.

She tried her spells one by one

Even every potion

She ever knew –

Nothing worked.

She tried once more

Much, much harder

And a lot longer.

Nothing worked

She tried in vain.

Even with a bottle

Of old sticking glue,

Then some cement –

She placed on her teeth

From where they fell –

All to no avail.

Other teeth fell

As she glued, cemented in the others.

Soon her face and mouth were covered,

Full of glue and cement.

She spat out as much as she could.

Right there on the floor.

With one tooth missing –

She began to search.

But, a second too late

For her friend the rat

Had gotten it first.

Angry and furious,

She kicked her friend

Rat went flying across the room

Banging into the door.

The witch didn't know what to do,

Then like a flash,

She remembered the Good Witch,

And thought to herself,

" Maybe Good Witch can save my teeth.

Make me pretty and mean again."

"But not like this!" she said out loud.

"A simple spell for just one day.

A simple spell with toad, newt

And whimpering rose. Will form my disguise -

Make me pretty for one day."

The spell was cast,

And with a puff of smoke –

Stood the prettiest lady

One had ever seen.

Except for one of her

Missing front teeth.

She grabbed Rat,

Shoved him into her pocket.

Ran outside, grabbing her magic broom.

Sat upon it, then screamed out,

"Off to the Good Witch's house!"

Some time later,

The witch landed in a small forest.

The forest was not far from the Good Witch's house.

She walked up to the Good Witch's front gate,

Where the smell of flowers filled the air.

She began to sneeze, "achoo! achoo! achooooo!"

"I hate flowers", said the Bad Witch.

She wiped her nose with her blouse's sleeve,

Opened the white gate, walked up the front door, and then rang the small bell.

Honey Dew barked,

Then all went quiet.

The door slowly opened,

The Good Witch said, "Hello, how can I help you?"

The Pretty Witch replied,

"My teeth are loose, help me you will"

The Good Witch replied, "Oh yes! We will see. At least I can try.

Please do step inside."

The Pretty Witch did so,

The door closed shut.

Around a table they both sat.

Honey Dew lying upon her mat,

One eye open, sniffing away as if something wasn't quite right.

The Good Witch said, "I see you're missing a tooth right in front –

One of your top ones." Then she asked, "Do you know where it is?"

The Pretty Witch replied, "It fell out this morning

And my Rrrrrrr…Oops!!

It fell on the floor, I couldn't find it."

Honey Dew looked on with both eyes open.

"Oh I see", said the Good Witch, "Please do wait a minute."

The Good Witch stood up, and,

Walked out the room.

Honey Dew looked at the Pretty Witch.

Sniffing and standing with her tail in a curl.

The Good Witch returned

With a very small wooden box.

She opened the lid which made a small squeak.

Then came a squeak from the Pretty Witch's pocket.

Honey Dew barked, the Good Witch said, "Quiet!"

The Good Witch handed the Pretty Witch

A dried up Daisy petal which was white.

She said, "Now place this where your tooth is missing

And close your mouth for 90 seconds. Let's hope you will see something fine."

90 seconds passed, the Pretty Witch opened her mouth,

Lo and behold! There once again stood a fine white tooth.

"It's only temporary", said the Good Witch,

"That's until you find the missing tooth, which you can replace the Daisy petal tooth,

Then all will be fine", she said.

The Pretty Witch smiled just like the sun.

"Now", said the Good Witch.

"Place one drop of this for every loose tooth."

With her tongue, the Pretty Witch counted all her loose teeth.

14 in total. But, 15 drops she dripped in her mouth.

"Now close your mouth for one and a quarter minutes", said the Good Witch.

The Pretty Witch did so, her eyes began bulging out of her head.

After one and a quarter minutes, she grasped for breath.

After catching it, ran her fingers along all of her teeth.

Pushing and pulling each and every tooth.

She smiled, pretty as a picture, and then asked, "How did you do that?"

"It's a secret potion", the Good Witch replied. "I'm sorry I cannot say."

"Oh yes you will!", said the Pretty Witch.

Then with a stamp of her foot, the Pretty Witch once again turned into

The bad, wart nosed witch.

Her rat jumped out of her pocket,

Unto the table, snarling at the Good Witch.

The Good Witch reached over to a side bench,

Picked up a small dish which on it lay some blackberry leaves,

Cinnamon, and fresh rose thorns.

She threw the contents towards Honey Dew,

Who then sparkled like the glistening rays of the sun.

Honey Dew had grown 20 feet tall. The Good Witch commanded, "be gone!"

Honey Dew leapt, and with one great bite, the Bad Witch was gone.

Honey Dew then chased the rat which was clearly no match.

With one quick snap, the rat had disappeared.

Honey Dew sat and slowly shrank down back to her normal size.

She barked with a smile, wagged her tail, then-

Spat out a tooth

– this was the missing tooth from you know who!

The Good Witch picked up the tooth,

Walked over to the rubbish bin, opened the lid, and

While slowly dropping the tooth inside, she said,

"Oh well! One for the tooth fairy."

CPSIA information can be obtained
at www.ICGtesting.com
Printed in the USA
BVXC01n1604040914
365429BV00004B/10

9 781496 984920